Thank You

Thank You

pictures
Sam Usher

words
Joseph Coelho

Frances Lincoln
Children's Books

Tatenda said thank you every day
to everyone whenever he could.

Thank you to Mum and Dad
for making breakfast.

Thank you to the post lady for delivering his favourite comic.

Thank you to his teacher for marking his work.

Thank you to the shop assistants for stacking the shelves.

But lately, it seemed
that no one could hear his thank you.
Their heads were foggy with worry
and clouded with fear.

So Tatenda decided to say
his biggest thank you ever.
He stood on tiptoe
and stretched his arms
high over his head, and
the thank you in him bubbled.

He brought his arms down wide
like a huge rainbow,
big enough to hug the entire world,
and the thank you in him fizzed...

and this time...

Tatenda's thank you came out different.

He could see it.
His thank you floated
around the kitchen
and zipped out the front door.

Tatenda, Mum and Dad followed it
past the post lady
who smiled when she saw it,
and the post lady's smile
made the thank you grow
and glow.

Tatenda, Mum, Dad and the post lady
chased the thank you to school where all
the teachers and children gasped when they
saw it, and it grew on their gasps and a little
of the sparkle from the teachers' eyes
shone within it.

Tatenda, Mum, Dad, the post lady, the teachers
and the children chased the thank you
to the local market where all the stall holders
gazed up and laughed as it floated by,
getting bigger on their chuckles
and giggling as it went.

The thank you drifted into
the branches of a huge oak tree
and got stuck!

Tatenda, Mum, Dad, the post lady,
the teachers, the children and the stall
holders tried to get it down with selfie
sticks, umbrellas and walking canes.

Nothing worked.

So, they made a ladder
of bodies for Tatenda to climb.
He caught hold of an edge of
the thank you and everyone...

pulled!

And the thank you...

popped!

A ribbon of thank yous
danced away on
the wind.

Some whisked by the bakers
where they rose and sweetened
like hot buns.

Some flew by the doctors
where they got bolder
and braver.

Some of the thank yous
landed by the dustbin men
and ballooned and sang.

By the end of the day the thank yous had left traces of themselves
everywhere, leaving a little bit of their colour and joy
around the whole town as they

bobbed by nurses,
hovered by
road sweepers,

flickered
by librarians,

wafted by builders, and rolled around bus drivers.

As the sun set that evening
everyone went home
with a little thank you
nestled in their hearts.

And as Mum and Dad
tucked Tatenda into bed
they whispered...

'Goodnight Tatenda
and thank YOU.'

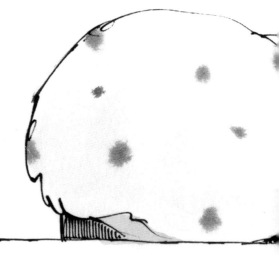

about the book

I wrote this story during the year of the coronavirus pandemic. It meant we had to stay inside for weeks on end, without doing any of the things we normally do: visiting places like the library, going to work or school, or even simply seeing friends and family.

However, hearing the NHS clap on a Thursday evening very quickly became a wonderful marker of the weeks. I'd open my window and listen and join in as pans were battered and people out-of-sight hollered. In that moment there was and is something magical as communities come together in a simple act of gratitude, not just for doctors and nurses but for the shop assistants, postal workers, bus drivers and other people that help us all in our daily lives. In writing Tatenda's story I wanted to honour that feeling and underline the power in gratitude, a power that is available to us all, old and young, big and small.

Thank you.

Joseph Coelho

By buying a copy of this book, you have made a donation of 3% of the retail price to Groundwork UK.

Groundwork supports the communities that need the most help. We want to create a clean and green future where every community is strong and everyone has a chance to be happy. We've been helping people deal with the impact of coronavirus since the pandemic began. For example, in association with Comic Relief we've offered grants to provide emergency relief to the communities that need it most.

Thank you for your donation to Groundwork!

Brimming with creative inspiration, how-to projects, and useful information to enrich your everyday life, Quarto Knows is a favourite destination for those pursuing their interests and passions. Visit our site and dig deeper with our books into your area of interest: Quarto Creates, Quarto Cooks, Quarto Homes, Quarto Lives, Quarto Drives, Quarto Explores, Quarto Gifts, or Quarto Kids.

First published in 2020 by Frances Lincoln Children's Books, an imprint of The Quarto Group.
The Old Brewery, 6 Blundell Street, London N7 9BH, United Kingdom.
T (0)20 7700 6700 F (0)20 7700 8066 www.QuartoKnows.com

ISBN 978-0-7112-6203-4

The illustrations were created in ink and watercolour
Set in Mrs Ant

Published and edited by Katie Cotton
Art direction by Mike Jolley
Production by Beth Sweeney

Manufactured in the UK at CPI 092020
1 3 5 7 9 10 8 6 4 2